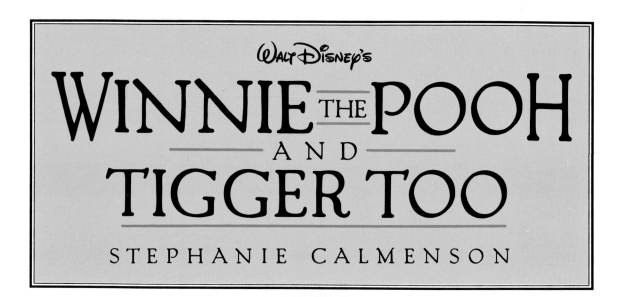

Walt Disney's

WINNIE THE POOH
AND
TIGGER TOO

STEPHANIE CALMENSON

DISNEY PRESS

NEW YORK

Illustrations by Vaccaro Associates, Inc.
Layout by Ennis McNulty
Painted by Lou Paleno

"The Wonderful Thing About Tiggers"
Words and Music by
Richard M. Sherman and Robert B. Sherman
Copyright © 1964 Wonderland Music Company, Inc.
Copyright Renewed.
All Rights Reserved. Used by Permission.

FIRST EDITION

1   3   5   7   9   10   8   6   4   2

Library of Congress Catalog Card Number: 93-73813
ISBN: 1-56282-630-1

Walt Disney's

WINNIE THE POOH
AND
TIGGER TOO

One fine day in the Hundred-Acre Wood, Winnie the Pooh was sitting on a comfortable log in his Thoughtful Spot when suddenly his thoughts were interrupted by a sound he knew very well: *BOING! BOING! BOING!*

"Hello, Pooh! It's me, Tigger!" exclaimed Tigger, bounding into the Thoughtful Spot and bouncing Pooh right off his log. "T-I–double Guh–Er spells Tigger!"

"Yes, I know," said Pooh. "You've bounced me before."

Tigger jumped up and shook Pooh's hand. "Well, I'd better be going now. I have a lot more bouncing to do."

Nearby, Piglet was busy sweeping up outside his house. He began to hear a noise, which started off smaller than Piglet himself but quickly grew larger and larger. Suddenly the noise turned into Tigger, who bounced Piglet right off his feet.

"Ooh, Tigger. You scared me!" said Piglet.

"I did? But I gave you one of my littlest bounces. I'm saving my biggest one for old long ears," Tigger said. He pulled up his ears as far as they would go, trying to look like Rabbit.

"Well, I'm glad I got one of your little bounces. Thank you, Tigger," said Piglet. He waved good-bye as Tigger bounced off down the road in the direction of Rabbit's house.

"There, that should do it," said Rabbit as he gathered up an armload of carrots from his garden. But then he heard a sound he knew all too well: *BOING! BOING! BOING!*

"Oh no!" cried Rabbit. "Stop!"

But Tigger didn't stop. He bounced Rabbit right off his feet, sending the carrots flying every which way.

"Hello, Rabbit! It's me, Tigger," said Tigger. "That's T-I–double Guh–Er..."

"Oh, please, please! Don't spell it," moaned Rabbit, sitting up and pushing Tigger away. "Oh, Tigger, won't you ever stop bouncing?"

"Why would I? Bouncing is what Tiggers do best. Hoo-hoo-*hoo*!" exclaimed Tigger. He started to sing:

> *Oh, the wonderful thing about Tiggers*
> *is Tiggers are wonderful things.*
> *Their tops are made out of rubber,*
> *and their bottoms are made of springs.*
> *They're bouncy, trouncy, flouncy, pouncy,*
> *fun, fun, fun, fun, fun.*
> *But the most wonderful thing about*
> *Tiggers is that I'm the only one!*

As Tigger bounced away, Rabbit stomped angrily around his garden, gathering up his scattered carrots. "Something must be done about that Tigger!" he said to himself.

That afternoon Rabbit invited Pooh and Piglet to a meeting at his house.

"I say Tigger is getting too bouncy these days," Rabbit began. "Now, I've got a splendid idea. We'll take Tigger on an expedition to someplace he's never been. And then we'll lose him!"

"Lose him?" Pooh repeated. Losing someone didn't sound to him like a very friendly thing to do.

"Oh, we'll find him again the next morning," said Rabbit. "But by then he'll be a humble Tigger. A small and sad Tigger. An oh-Rabbit-am-I-glad-to-see-you Tigger. It will take those bounces right out of him." He rubbed his hands together eagerly.

The next morning crept into the Hundred-Acre Wood in a cold and misty sort of way. As Rabbit, Piglet, Pooh, and Tigger set off on their expedition, the mist was so thick that they could hardly see their feet at the ends of their legs.

Tigger bounced in circles around the others. He bounced ahead and came back again. Finally, he bounced off into some especially thick mist beside the trail, where he seemed to disappear.

"Quick," Rabbit said eagerly. "Now's our chance to lose him."

He ran into a hollow log and pulled Pooh and Piglet in behind him. Then he peeked out from inside the log and breathed a sigh of relief. Tigger was nowhere in sight.

"My splendid idea worked perfectly," Rabbit said with a chuckle. "Now we can all go home."

Pooh was very glad to hear that they were going home. "Yum, yum, time for lunch," he said.

"Halloo!" called a voice from not very far away.

"Oh no! It's you-know-who!" cried Rabbit. Before Pooh quite knew what was happening, Rabbit had grabbed him and pulled him back inside the log.

A second later Tigger bounced onto the very log where Rabbit, Piglet, and Pooh were hiding. "Halloo!" he shouted to the right. "Halloo!" he shouted to the left. Then he leaned down and shouted "Halloo!" right into the log.

Rabbit, Piglet, and Pooh shook all over as Tigger's shout echoed inside. But they didn't say a word.

Tigger hopped off the log and bounced away into the Hundred-Acre Wood, still calling, "Halloo!"

Rabbit jumped out of the log. "Hooray!" he cried. "We've done it! We've lost Tigger! We can go home now."

So they started off toward home.

"It's funny how everything looks the same in the mist," said Rabbit a few minutes later. "Take this sand pit, for instance. I'm sure we've seen it before."

"I'm sure you're right," said Pooh agreeably.

They kept walking, and in a little while they came upon the very same sand pit.

"Er…Rabbit? How would it be if as soon as we're out of sight of this old pit we try to find it again?" suggested Pooh. "Because, you see, we keep looking for home. But we keep finding this pit. So perhaps if we looked for this pit, we might find home."

"I don't see much sense in that," said Rabbit. "If I walked away from this pit and then walked back to it, of course I would find it again. Wait right here and I'll prove it to you."

With great determination, Rabbit set off into the mist. Pooh and Piglet sat down in the sand pit to wait for him to return.

They waited…and waited…and waited. Piglet fell fast asleep, leaning against Pooh's tummy. Suddenly he was awakened by a grumbling noise.

"What was that?" asked Piglet, jumping up.

"Why, I believe that was my tummy rumbling," said Pooh. "I'm awfully hungry. I think we should go home and have lunch."

"Do you know the way, Pooh?" asked Piglet.

"Well, I have twelve pots of honey in my cupboard that my tummy very much wants to find. So we can simply follow my tummy home," Pooh explained.

Piglet tried to be as quiet as possible so that Pooh's tummy could concentrate. Then, just as Piglet began to know where he was—

BOING! BOING! BOING!

It was Tigger! He bounced into Pooh and Piglet, rolling them over and over.

"Hello there, you two!" he said. "Where have you been?"

"We've been trying to find our way back home," said Pooh.

"But we seem to have lost Rabbit somewhere in the mist," added Piglet.

"Leave it to me," said Tigger. "I'll bounce him out of there in no time!"

At that very moment Rabbit was just about as lost as a Rabbit could be. He was so scared that he was trembling from the tops of his ears all the way down to the tips of his toes. Little noises that he wouldn't even have noticed on a sunny day with his friends suddenly sounded loud and frightening. Soon Rabbit was so scared that he couldn't stand it anymore. He ran away as fast as his legs would carry him.

He wasn't looking where he was going and ran straight into...

"Tigger!" cried Rabbit. "You're supposed to be lost!" Rabbit couldn't remember ever being so happy to see Tigger before.

"Lost? Tiggers never get lost," said Tigger. "Come on, Rabbit. Let's go home. Hang on."

Tigger placed his tail in Rabbit's hand, then bounced off toward home. Rabbit held on tight as he was carried along through the mist and the mud. He was now a thoroughly humiliated Rabbit. A lost-and-found Rabbit. A why-oh-why-do-these-things-happen-to-me Rabbit.

But more than anything else, he was a happy-to-be-going-home Rabbit.

A short while after Rabbit's getting-lost adventure, it began to snow in the Hundred-Acre Wood. The snow fell quietly all night long. In the morning a soft white blanket cozily covered all the houses in the forest, including the house where Kanga and her baby, Roo, lived.

"Mama, when is Tigger going to get here?" asked Roo.

"Be patient, dear," said Kanga as she swept a path through the snow. "He'll be here soon."

Almost before the words were out of her mouth, Kanga and Roo heard a familiar sound:

BOING! BOING! BOING!

Tigger slid into the yard, creating a wave of snow that knocked Roo right off the mailbox.

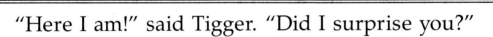

"Here I am!" said Tigger. "Did I surprise you?"

"You sure did!" said Roo. "I like surprises. I like bouncing, too."

"I know," said Tigger. "That's why I'm here. I've come to take you bouncing with me."

"Hooray!" said Roo. "I'm all ready."

Roo and Tigger said good-bye to Kanga, and then Tigger led the way out of the yard with his great big bounces:

BOING! BOING! BOING!

And Roo followed right behind with his very little ones:

BOING! BOING! BOING!

When Tigger and Roo had gone a short distance into the forest, Tigger called, "Hey, look, Roo. It's old long ears."

Sure enough, Roo spotted Rabbit up ahead, gliding happily across a frozen pond. In fact, Rabbit was enjoying his skating so much that he didn't even see Tigger and Roo.

"Can Tiggers ice-skate?" asked Roo. "As fancy as Mr. Rabbit can?"

"Oh-ho-ho!" said Tigger. "Ice-skating is what Tiggers do best. Watch!"

Tigger bounced onto the pond. "Whee! This is easy," he said as he slid across the ice. First he skated on one foot, then the other. Next he tried to skate on the tip of his tail. That's when he started wiggling…

…and wobbling…

…and sliding faster and faster across the ice—straight toward Rabbit.

"Look out!" Tigger cried. "I can't stop!"

When Rabbit turned and saw Tigger heading his way, his eyes grew very wide. He threw up his hands. "No! No! Don't!" he shouted.

But Tigger, who had very little choice in the matter, just kept on coming. He crashed right into Rabbit, then slid into the snow. Rabbit went flying through the front door of his house, knocking over everything inside.

"Why does it always have to be me?" moaned Rabbit. "Why, oh why, oh why?"

"Yech," Tigger said, spitting out a mouthful of snow. "Tiggers do *not* like ice-skating."

Tigger and Roo left Rabbit and bounced farther into the Hundred-Acre Wood. "I bet you're good at climbing trees, huh, Tigger?" asked Roo.

"Hoo-hoo-*hoo*!" laughed Tigger. "That's what Tiggers do best. Only Tiggers don't climb trees, they bounce them. Come on, I'll show you!"

With Roo sitting on his shoulders, Tigger bounced from branch to branch to branch up to the very tippity-top of the very tallest tree he could find.

"Pretty good bouncing, huh?" said Tigger, looking down. But when he saw how far he was from the ground, he wrapped his arms around the tree trunk and closed his eyes tight. "Wait just a minute! How did this tree get so high?" Suddenly he felt a tug on the end of his tail and looked down to see that Roo was swinging back and forth from the end of it.

"S-s-stop that, kid, please," begged Tigger. "You're rocking the forest!"

While Tigger was busy getting stuck in the tree, Pooh and Piglet were busy tracking some footprints around a bush. They stopped when they heard a loud "Hallooooo!"

"L-look, Piglet," said Pooh. "There's something in that tree over there."

"Hallooooo!" called the voice again.

"Pooh! Piglet!" called a second, smaller voice.

When he looked more carefully, Pooh saw that the some-thing in the tree was Tigger and Roo. "Hello," said Pooh. "What are you two doing up there?"

"Well, I'm all right," said Roo. "But Tigger's stuck."

"Help! Somebody! Please, help!" cried Tigger. "Get Christopher Robin!"

It wasn't long before Christopher Robin arrived, with Kanga and Rabbit right behind him.

"My goodness," said Kanga, looking up. "How did you get way up there, Roo?"

"It was easy, Mama. We bounced up," said Roo. "But now Tigger's stuck."

"That's too bad," said Kanga.

"No, that's good," said Rabbit happily. "Tigger can't bounce anybody as long as he's stuck up in that tree."

"We can't just leave him up there. We have to get them both down," said Christopher Robin firmly. "Now, everyone take hold of my coat. Ready? Okay, you're first, Roo. Jump!"

"Try not to fall too fast, dear," Kanga said.

"Here I come. Whee!" cried Roo as he tumbled down through the air. He landed safely in the middle of Christopher Robin's coat, then popped up into Kanga's arms.

"That was fun!" said Roo. "Come on, Tigger. Jump!"

"Jump? Tiggers don't jump. They bounce," said Tigger, clutching the tree tighter than ever.

"Then why don't you bounce down," suggested Pooh.

"Don't be ridiculous. Tiggers only bounce *up*," said Tigger.

"Then you'll have to climb down," said Christopher Robin.

"Tiggers can't climb down because...because their tails get in the way," said Tigger. He wrapped his tail tightly around the tree trunk.

"That settles it," said Rabbit. "If Tigger won't jump down or climb down, we'll just have to leave him up there forever!"

"Forever?" moaned Tigger. "Oh, if I ever get down from this tree, I promise never to bounce again."

"I heard that!" cried Rabbit, jumping for joy. "Did you all hear that? Tigger promised never to bounce again!"

"All right, Tigger," Christopher Robin called up to him. "It's time for you to come down now."

It took some more coaxing, but finally Tigger unwound his tail from the tree and slo-o-o-owly and carefully climbed down.

As soon as his feet touched the ground, Tigger was his old cheerful self again. "Hey, I'm so happy to be out of that tree, I feel like bouncing!" he cried.

"No, no, no!" Rabbit said quickly. "You promised! No more bouncing."

"Uh-oh. I did promise, didn't I?" said Tigger. "Does that really mean I can never ever bounce again? Not even one teensy-weensy bounce?"

"Not even a smidgen of a bounce," said Rabbit.

Tigger's tail flopped. His shoulders dropped. He walked off sadly into the softly falling snow.

Tigger's friends watched him go. Rabbit was the only one with a smile on his face.

Roo tugged on Christopher Robin's coat. "Christopher Robin," he said, "I like the old bouncy Tigger best."

"So do I, Roo," said Christopher Robin.

"Me, too," said Piglet, and Pooh nodded.

"We all do," said Kanga. "Don't you agree, Rabbit?"

"Well," said Rabbit. "I...ah..." He thought about all the times Tigger had bounced him off his feet.

"Yes, Rabbit?" said Pooh.

"Well, you see," said Rabbit. "I...ah..." He thought about how sad Tigger had looked walking off without his bounce.

"Oh, all right," said Rabbit at last. "I guess I like the old Tigger better, too."

"Oh boy!" shouted Tigger, who had heard Rabbit from far away. He returned with a quick bounce and knocked Rabbit off his feet. "You mean I can have my bounce back?" He picked Rabbit up and hugged him. "Come on, Rabbit. Let's bounce together!"

Rabbit couldn't believe his ears. "Me? Bounce?" he said.

"Well, sure," said Tigger. "Look, you've got the feet for it."

"I do?"

Everyone looked down at Rabbit's feet. No one had ever noticed before what good bouncing feet they were.

Rabbit tried a little bounce…then a bigger one…then a bigger one than that. Before long he was bouncing just like Tigger. A smile spread across Rabbit's face.

"Well, come on, everybody!" he said.

So Pooh, Piglet, Kanga, Roo, Tigger, Rabbit, and Christopher Robin happily bounced together all through the Hundred-Acre Wood.